Matthew Looney's Voyage To The Earth

Other Avon Camelot Books by
Jerome Beatty, Jr.

JEROME BEATTY, JR. has written several books for young people. A former newspaperman and magazine editor, his articles have appeared in many publications, including *The Saturday Review*, where he wrote the Trade Winds column. Born in New York, Mr. Beatty was graduated from Dartmouth College. He now lives on Cape Cod with his family.

Matthew Looney's Voyage To The Earth

A space story by JEROME BEATTY, JR.

Illustrated by GAHAN WILSON

AN AVON CAMELOT BOOK

AVON BOOKS
A division of
The Hearst Corporation
959 Eighth Avenue
New York, New York 10019

Copyright © MCMLXI by Jerome Beatty, Jr.
Published by arrangement with Addison-Wesley Publishing Co., Inc.
Library of Congress Catalog Card Number: 61-2909
ISBN: 0-380-01494-7

First Camelot Printing, February, 1972

CAMELOT TRADEMARK REG. U.S. PAT. OFF. AND
FOREIGN COUNTRIES, REGISTERED TRADEMARK—
MARCA REGISTRADA, HECHO EN U.S.A.

Printed in the U.S.A.

10

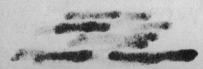

TABLE OF CONTENTS

"The Moon is considered to be completely life-less."—Otto Binder. *Planets: Other worlds of our solar system.* Golden Press, New York. 1959.

". . . the Moon is an uncomfortable place to be in . . ."—H. A. Rey. *The Stars: A new way to see them.* Houghton Mifflin, Boston. 1952.

"The Moon is certainly an unpleasant place."—Franklyn M. Branley. *The Moon: Earth's natural satellite.* T. Y. Crowell, New York. 1960.

"Earth is a dead planet, and always will be."—Robinson K. Russo, Lu. D. *Our Useless Neighbor.* Mooniversity Press, Crater Copernicus. 4M?o.

To the Unborn Cabin Boys of Space

I

The Powder Factory

It was breakfast time on the Moon.

"Matt! Matthew Looney!" Mrs. Looney cried. "Now where can that boy be?" She set a dish of cold Syzygies in front of little Maria Looney, who looked up at her mother and tattled.

"I know where big brother is. He's probably back there, reading that magazine again."

Mrs. Looney sighed as she wiped her hands on her apron and started off to look for her son. Like everyone else, the Looney family lived underground. They occupied a comfortable cave in the town of Crater Plato. There was a spare room and bath where young Matt usually went into hiding when he wanted to be alone. The very minute his mother was calling him, the boy was there, stretched out on the bed, busy reading the latest issue of *Northern Lights,* with the stone door shut tight so no one would bother him. No wonder he didn't hear his name called.

The story Matt was reading was titled "Is There Life on Earth?" and it had been written by Captain Lockhard Looney, one of the greatest heroes of the Moon, and Matt's own uncle. It so happened that there were two things that interested Matt the most at this point: one was his Uncle Lucky, and the other was outer space, especially the satellite known as Earth.

Some people thought these were the two things that interested Uncle Lucky the most, too, for he didn't seem to be happy unless he was discovering new places and winning new medals for himself. The great pilot-scientist-author, in his search for knowledge of outer space, had explored such territories as Venus,

Reading the latest issue of Northern Lights . . .

Mars, and the Astroidal Belt. He had found no living creatures. Now, he was saying in the article in *Northern Lights*, there was one last place to go. Matt read:

> We must take a new look at the funny-looking, lopsided object we call the Earth. According to all the studies made by our scientists, it can support no life. Wrapped in a blanket of deadly oxygen, spinning dizzily, exposed to the poisonous rays of sunlight—it is an unpleasant place. But we must remember we were wrong about the Sun, when for many years we considered it ice-cold, and we could be wrong about Earth. Therefore, my next expedition will be to that mysterious body, and for that purpose the spaceship *Moonbeam II* is rapidly being completed. Supplies will be gathered and a crew of volunteers organized and trained for the journey.

"Boy!" Matt said to himself, and he pictured himself on the flight deck of the *Moonbeam II* as she took off for space. Just then a familiar voice broke into his daydream.

"Come on, son," his mother said as she entered the room. "Your food is ready, and your father

4

is home and wants to talk to you about what you're going to do now that summer vacation has begun."

They walked through the cool corridors together until they reached the dining room, where Maria was finishing up her dessert and Monroe Looney, Matt's father, was also seated. He was a big, healthy man. He and Matt greeted each other warmly. One thing about the Moon— everyone is always cheerful. The main reason is that if you frown or look unhappy, it hurts your face. If you become angry, you get a sore throat. It's got something to do with the atmosphere.

"Well, Matt," his father said, "I've got a job all lined up for you at the powder factory this summer. And tonight's the night I'm going to take you over there and show you around. How do you like that?" He leaned back and smiled.

Matt looked at his plate and didn't speak.

His mother paused on her way to the kitchen and asked, "Well, Matt, aren't you going to answer your father?"

"There has always been a powder factory, and there will always be a powder factory."

Matt finally looked up. "Dad, I don't want to work in the powder factory."

"Well, what do you want to do then, play mumblety-peg all summer?"

The boy took a deep breath. "I want to go to Earth with Uncle Lucky."

Matt's mother screamed. His sister giggled. His father yelled, "What? You've been reading those space books again!"

There was a moment of silence. Finally Mr. Looney spoke again, in a serious tone.

"Young man, when I was your age I took a job in the powder factory and today I am manager of the business. I can't think of any better training for a boy than to start as I did. Somehow the young people these days spend all their time thinking about space travel and stuff like that which doesn't do anyone any good.

"There has always been a powder factory, and there always will be a powder factory, long after your Uncle Lucky is forgotten. That's where you'll be this summer, and not on some foolish trip to a dead planet. Now, if you'll get ready, we'll be on our way to the Mount Pico Powder Works."

Matt and his father smiled at each other, the way folks do on the Moon even when they are not entirely happy, and a few minutes later they had left home and Crater Plato behind them, and were trudging around the edge of the Sea of Showers and approaching the huge mass of crumbly stuff which was Mount Pico. There, in an immense cave, was where the machinery and men were located. In spite of himself, Matt was fascinated by the activity. He had never been inside the place before.

A tremendous machine—with great grinders, rollers, choppers, and smashers—was operating noisily. At one end gangs of workmen were feeding the machine with a variety of objects, from the other end emerged a steady stream of powder. Conveyer belts carried it away out of sight.

Mr. Looney put one arm on his son's shoulders and waved with the other. "This is it," he said proudly.

8

A tremendous machine was operating noisily .

"Why is it so important, Dad?"

"I'm glad you asked," replied his father. He went on to discuss a subject dear to his heart. "As we all know, because of the marvelous living conditions on the Moon, nothing wears out. If we were on your favorite heavenly body —Earth—for example, we would find that because of the large amount of water in the atmosphere and on the ground, and with the wind blowing all the time, things would crumble and rot away after a while. Not on the Moon, though.

"One slight problem here is that when we don't want a thing any more, we have to find some means of disposing of it. Before the invention of the powder gin, people just dumped everything into spots such as the Sea of Crisis or the uninhabited Crater Arzachel. The Moon was cluttered up with junk until this marvelous machine was developed. Now everything is simply ground up into dust and spread around in the Carpathian Mountains and places like that."

"What's that big thing going in now?" asked Matt, pointing to the mouth of the machine.

"That's a home, Matt, one of those real old-fashioned caves nobody wants to live in any more. And look, there goes the furniture too. A sofa, a saxophone, a bundle of neckties. To-morrow is our busiest day of the week. That's when we take garbage and ladies' dresses."

The two watched as the machinery ate up all the material and, with a roar, spewed it out the other end onto the conveyers which, Mr. Looney explained, carried the powder to various corners of the Moon where it was out of the way. For the rest of the day Matt visited the offices, the repair shops, the cafeteria, and other sections of the plant under the guidance of his father, the manager. As they finally left to go home, Matt had to admit to himself that it had been an interesting experience, and he decided that he ought to admit it to his father too.

"That was fun, Dad."

His father, who had been telling the boy every amusing or exciting story about the powder factory that he could recall, was pleased to hear his son's remark.

He looked up at the huge, peculiar blue-and-white Earth hanging in the black sky and said, "Son, Earth isn't even worth looking at, so why visit it? It's such an ugly and uninteresting sight that ordinary people and astronomers both, when they gaze at the heavens, turn their telescopes on much prettier planets and stars. Hardly anyone thinks there are intelligent beings on Earth, and a lot of people are beginning to wonder about the great Lucky Looney, ever since he began all this talk about the *Moonbeam II* expedition. As much as I admire my brother Lockhard, I don't want my son mixed up in this scheme of his. Besides, they won't be taking any fellows your age along."

"But, Dad, I read in *Northern Lights* there was a cabin boy's job open. I could apply for that."

Mr. Looney stopped in the middle of Crater Plato's main street and looked at his son. "Matthew, you haven't been listening to me. You're going to work in the powder factory, starting next Moonday, and that's final."

"*Astronomers turn their telescopes on much prettier
planets and stars.*"

They turned and walked the rest of the way home in silence. Matt had stopped smiling and his face hurt, from frowning. Mr. Looney felt his throat starting to itch.

II

Uncle Lucky Saves Maria

The following evening Matt and Maria had to go to bowling lessons. She carried the big black bowling ball as he took her by the hand and led her out into the roads of Crater Plato. There was no sun shining—for its bright, hot rays were considered dangerous. They caused a disease known as *cosmos*.

Little Maria must have been thinking about this, because she looked up at her brother and asked, "Why can't I ever go out when the sun is shining?"

"Because you get cosmos, that's why," he answered in a slightly disgusted tone. "It makes your skin change color."

"Did you ever have that?"

"Yes, once." Matt smiled a bit, as they walked along. "I went hunting and I didn't start back quick enough. The sun came up and it made me feel all sleepy. I lay down in some sand and it was soft and warm. I was running it through my fingers and just lying there, when they came and got me."

Maria's eyes popped. "You mean the Kidcatchers came?"

Matt nodded his head. Almost every day you can hear the sirens as the squads of Kidcatchers race out to bring back the youngsters who have wandered away and become stranded someplace where they are exposed to cosmos. Most of these children sneak out on purpose because, like a lot of other things, it may be bad for you but it's an awful lot of fun!

As you grow older on the Moon, you learn that cosmos is really a terrible way to suffer and

"*Because you get cosmos, that's why.*"

you are very careful to step outside only when the sun is gone. That's why people eat breakfast at night, eat dinner when they come home in the morning, and stay indoors and sleep during daylight. If they catch a case of cosmos by mistake, the only cure is to stay home until it goes away.

As brother and sister went along, there was plenty of earthshine to light their way to the bowling teacher's cave twenty miles away in nearby Crater Archimedes. Twenty miles is an easy distance on the Moon, where gravity is so weak that walking is a cinch. Unlike large, important planets such as Jupiter and Neptune, the Moon is so small that its force of gravity is barely strong enough to hold things to its surface. Walking, then, is just a matter of pushing gently with your toes and sort of gliding along.

As a matter of fact, next to cosmos, the other big problem on the Moon is *velocipitis*. This is a condition caused by people who walk too fast, or who forget themselves and jump up too fast from a chair, for instance. They simply start

Velocipitis *is a condition caused by jumping up too fast from
a chair, for instance.*

climbing away from the ground, and unless they can catch hold of something, it takes a long time for gravity to bring them down again.

Like cosmos, it has always been very hard to teach youngsters about the dangers of velocipitis. What with the running and jumping and whooping and hollering that kids do, you'll often find them shooting off into the sky. Moon parents sometimes say they spend half their time standing around underneath their children, throwing ropes to them and trying to pull them down to *luna firma* ("solid Moon," if you are not up on your foreign languages).

Learning to walk right is very important for boys and girls. Until they've mastered the technique, about all you can do is watch them carefully, keeping them on a long leash, or else filling their pockets with some of the very heavy volcanic candy that is made just for the purpose. (Even if they swallow the candy, it is still doing the job, you see.) That's why bowling is such a popular game on the Moon, because it is fairly

20

safe from velocipitis. Hopscotch, on the other hand, is forbidden.

Matt, who was old enough to know all about this, must have had his mind on something else as he and his sister moseyed along. He looked at his watch.

"Gosh," he said to Maria, "we're going to be late. We'd better hurry. Here, let me carry the ball."

Maria handed the big ball in its carrying bag to her brother, and they both started hurrying down the streets in the outskirts of Archimedes. Matt moved with the correct knee-action motion which kept him from bouncing, but in her innocence Maria hopped and skipped. After a couple of skips she found herself climbing into the sky.

"Help, Matt, help!" she screamed, as she went sailing up over his head. Too far away to reach her, Matt stood there horrified, realizing what a boner he had pulled when he thoughtlessly had taken the heavy bowling ball—the bowling ball she was supposed to carry just to keep this from happening.

"What a dummy I am!" he groaned. He looked up and saw Maria, kicking her legs and waving her arms, and just floating in no special direction at all. She didn't have enough momentum to keep going up, but she couldn't come down. She was about thirty feet in the atmosphere, causing a terrible racket with her crying and screaming.

There were two ways out for poor Matt. He could notify the Rescue Squad, which had all the equipment—ladders, ropes, antigravitators. They would probably shoot a controlled balloon up to Maria and have her down in a second. Or he could try to bring her down himself, and avoid the scandal. While Matt deliberated, he saw a moving shadow down the road. Someone was coming!

"Oh, gosh," he said, "if you would just stop your yelling. Maria! Be quiet! I'll get you in a minute."

She kept up the racket, of course, and the un-

22

He saw Maria kicking her legs and waving her arms . . .

known intruder grew closer. Matt was feeling more helpless and gloomy than ever, when the person approaching took on a familiar appearance.

"Uncle Lucky!" Matt shouted. "It's you!"

A tall man with short-cropped white hair walked on the scene. He was wearing the uniform of an officer in the Space Navy, and he looked capable and athletic. From above him came a weak cry.

"Uncle Lucky, save me!" Maria kicked and waved.

"Well, Matt, my boy," Captain Looney's voice boomed out. "What can I do for you?" He glanced up. "I guess that's a silly question, hey, boy?" He laughed loudly. "What were you doing, Maria, playing hopscotch? You know that's against the law unless you have a license." He laughed some more. "Just you wait there, young lady. Don't go away."

Captain Looney chuckled at his humor, making Matt wonder when his uncle would quit the jokes and get down to business.

"Well, if we had a rope, it would be easy,"

said the Captain, scratching his chin. "We could call the Rescue Squad." He stopped and glanced at his nephew.

"But, Uncle Lucky, then Mother and Dad will find out. Isn't there some other way?"

"We'll think of something. What's this?" He picked up the bowling ball by the carrying handle. Matt explained how the accident had happened.

"Why, Matt," his uncle exclaimed. "You don't mean you took this from Maria! That's why you're in such a fix. You know the rule: never take anything from a small child without first giving him or her some object of at least equal weight. We wouldn't have any kids left on the Moon if folks didn't observe that rule carefully."

Matt looked unhappy.

"I'm only telling you this for your own good," his uncle continued. "If you are interested in space travel, you must remember the little things as well as the big ones. Well, it's all right, son. This is going to solve our problem for us."

From above came a wail. Uncle Lucky respond-

25

ed to it. "Now, Maria, do as I say. Keep perfectly still."

He balanced the ball on the tips of the fingers of one hand, slowly stretched it out to arm's length, and gave it a slight push upwards. The round object seemed to float toward Maria, moving ever so slowly and turning ever so gently.

"When that handle comes close enough," Captain Looney instructed, "do not move your arms or legs, but just carefully reach out your fingers and grasp it."

Matt watched with fascination as the ball went closer and closer to his sister's outstretched fingers. Finally it stopped moving, before it reached the girl, and then—in a few minutes—it began to come down again. Maria began to blubber.

Matt's heart fell. "Gee whiz!"

Uncle Lucky held up the palm of his hand. "Please, kids. All this means is that I'll do it the second time. Just like the trip to Mars. Missed it completely. Had to come back and try again."

With that, the ball came down onto his fingers and he slowly repeated the maneuver. This time

He balanced the ball on the tips of his fingers . . .

the ball floated accurately to where Maria could take hold of it and as she did so, it began to come down again, turning the poor girl upside down.

"Don't move!" cried Uncle Lucky. "Just hold it and take a deep breath."

There was a whishing noise as Maria inhaled.

"All right," said Uncle Lucky, "now look at the sky and blow! Hard!"

The girl's cheeks puffed out as she blew, and Matt saw that the jet action had caused her to move toward the ground a little bit. She did it again and moved faster. After a few more blows she was within reach, and her uncle pulled her down to safety.

"There," said her rescuer. "And Matt, remember that air-blowing trick. It's a good one. Saved me many a time from an embarrassing situation."

"But, Uncle Lucky, how come the ball floated down and Maria didn't?"

"Well, that's one of the mysteries of the Universe, Matt. A solid object like this round ball is affected more quickly than a person. Perhaps

Maria's kicking and yelling counteracted the force of gravity."

Maria, who was tightly holding her uncle's hand as they continued the trip to the bowling teacher's, said sadly, "I'm never going to kick or yell again in my whole life."

The other two laughed, and Captain Looney went on. "That's why we need to visit Earth so badly. We've just got to find out more about such matters." He turned to his nephew. "Say, why don't you try for the cabin boy's job on the expedition? It would be a fine start for your career as a space scientist."

Matt hung his head and kicked at a hunk of lava. "Dad wouldn't let me go anyway. He wants me to work in the powder factory. Gosh, Uncle Lucky, I don't want to be stuck there the rest of my life like Dad! I want to be a scientist, not a powder maker!"

"Just a minute, Matt, he isn't stuck there. The Mount Pico Powder Works is the best on the Moon, thanks to the excellent job being done by the manager—your father and my brother. It's only natural for him to want you to follow in his footsteps."

The trio had reached their destination. At the entrance to the cave was a sign:

ARCHIMEDES BOWLING ALLEY
Instruction by Miss Burns

Also at the entrance was Miss Burns, a large woman who showed her teeth and gushed, "Oh, Captain Looney, how nice of you to come along. Bowling, you know, is the safest sport on the Moon. We've never lost a student, as long as he's carried his bowling ball with him. Yes, we can almost say that we've conquered gravity with the bowling ball. You spacemen understand that, don't you? Remember our motto: 'Walk softly and carry a big bowling ball.'" She giggled and disappeared into the cave with Maria.

The Captain looked at Matt and said, "You almost spoiled her record, pal. Say, about the expedition, I'll talk to your father when I see him tomorrow. Maybe we can work out something."

30

Miss Burns was a large woman who gushed.

"Oh, boy, would you?"

"I can't guarantee anything. Also, another fellow has made application for the cabin boy's job already. Name's Hector Hornblower. Says he's a friend of yours. Well, I must be going." He patted Matt's shoulder and left.

Matt went on into Miss Burns's cave, his head pounding. Hector Hornblower! That kid! Friend? He was practically Matt's worst enemy and rival, ever since Matt had been made captain of the mumblety-peg team. Now he would go on the Earth expedition, maybe!

III

Studying at the Mooniversity

Matthew Looney stood at the kitchen counter the next day, opening a can of Cricket Ration. He put a few choice morsels in a dish, placed the can in the cupboard, and carried the dish back to his room where he set it before Ronald, his pet murtle. The Looney family was in its cave, waiting for the sun to go down, and Matt was feeding his pet and talking to it in an attempt to forget what was happening in the living room.

That's where his father and his uncle were discussing Matt's future, each trying to convince the other. Matt could hear their voices—and sometimes a burst of laughter—but he had no way of

33

knowing which way the argument was going, so he just played with his murtle, Ronald, and tried not to guess.

He had captured the animal a year before when his father had taken him on a camping trip to the Ocean of Storms, where Mr. Looney was seeking new powder disposal sites. Traveling through the deep, bone-dry canals to avoid the danger of falling meteorites which often pelt that area of the Moon, they had almost stepped on the tiny murtle. The creature was no bigger than a fist, and protected by a hard shell covering its back. It had apparently been separated from its mother.

"Look, Dad!" Matt had cried. At that, it had withdrawn its head and four feet into the shell and become like a large piece of lava, almost invulnerable. "What is it?"

His father had stopped and looked back. "Why, it's a murtle. I haven't seen one in ages. Here, you can always grab them by the tail. For some reason, they can't retract their tails as they can the rest of them."

34

So he just played with his murtle.

And that was how Matt caught Ronald and brought him back home, where he was the object of much curiosity, for one seldom sees a murtle in Crater Plato. Now he watched Ronald, who hadn't grown any larger since the day he was caught, gobble up the tasty murtle food.

"If I go to Earth, Ronald, I'll take you with me."

The boy jumped as a deep voice boomed out, "I don't think that will be possible, son." It was Uncle Lucky, who had stuck his head into the room to call Matt. "Come on in. We've made up our minds."

A few moments later Matt sat nervously in the living room as his father said, "I haven't changed my plans about your future in the powder works." Matt groaned to himself. "And your uncle admits he has no evidence that you are cut out to be a space scientist." Matt thought he was going to cry.

Uncle Lucky spoke. "So we think you yourself are the one to make the decision."

Matt jumped up, grinning. "Wonderful! I decide on space!"

"Not so fast," his father said. "We mean you must try them both. Now, I have agreed to let you enter the cabin boy competition. If you win the post—and if you succeed in the other space tests that are given at the same time—I'll give you permission to join the expedition. But next year you must give the powder business a chance. Is it a deal?"

The excited boy's whooping and yelling proved that he must have thought it the best deal in the universe. The noise brought his mother into the room.

"Oh, Monroe, do you really think it's safe?" she asked, after hearing the news. "A mere child going off in one of those dangerous rocket ships." She began to sniffle.

Captain Looney answered her. "Well, Diana, I do expect to return safely, you know. Besides, Matt must have nine nights of intensive study and tests at the Mooniversity before he will be seriously considered for the crew of the *Moonbeam II*. If he makes it, this 'mere child' will know more about taking good care of himself

37

in space than most anyone on the Moon."

"Yes, I suppose so, Lockhard. It's only natural for me to worry. Well, I'll go pack your valise, Matthew." She hurried off, dabbing her eyes.

Thus it was that, the following Moonday, Matt found himself speeding by moonorail toward the city of Crater Copernicus instead of punching a time clock as an apprentice at the Mount Pico Powder Works. The train raced across the Sea of Showers, climbed the Carpathian range, descended the other side, and slowed down for the first stop in the outskirts of Copernicus.

"Mooniversity Heights!" the conductor called.

Matt climbed out, looked up and down the platform, and finally saw a strange figure hurrying his way. It was a tiny man with a tremendous white beard. His face and the top of his bald head were a pleasant dark color, and he was dressed in a long green robe that stretched to his toes.

When the man called to him, Matt realized it must be Professor Theodore P. Ploozer, the

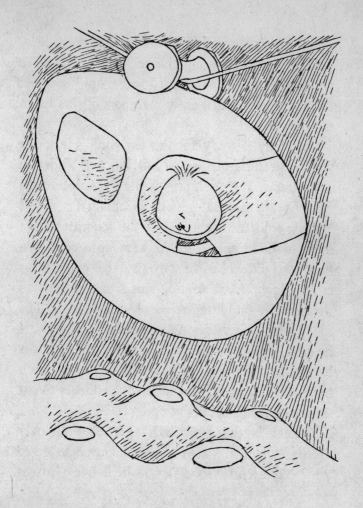

He found himself speeding by moonorail . . .

great astronomer-scientist who was to meet him. The professor was in charge of all the space projects at the Mooniversity and would conduct the examinations for crew members of this Earth expedition.

"My boy! How genice to see you!" He spoke with a peculiar accent. "I am Ploozer, and you will gestay at my house while in Copernicus. And how is my old gefriend Captain Looney?"

Matt told him briefly, but the scientist didn't seem to be listening, for he kept up a continual flow of talk while the two walked toward his cave which, Matt found, was situated next to the science building of the Mooniversity. The old professor was saying something about how he caught cosmos years ago, from being outdoors so much, studying the skies, and Matt was thinking how healthy the man looked. Suddenly Matt stopped short, his eyes popping.

"What is the gematter?" Professor Ploozer asked. "Oh, I know. You are surprised to gesee your old friend. Good news—he'll live with us too."

For there, in the doorway of the Ploozer residence, was none other than Hector Hornblower! He was smiling much more than necessary to keep his face from hurting; Matt knew the fellow was gloating. The two boys greeted each other.

"Hello, Matt."

"Hello, Heck."

Hector was a big boy, taller than Matt. Matt looked at him and thought, "He's too fat to get into a spaceship."

"All right, boys," the professor was shouting. "You have a getough schedule ahead of you. Better go to your rooms and get some sleep. Tomorrow night we gestart classes."

As the boys separated, Hector laughed and said, "You're too skinny to go to the Earth, Matt."

The next nine nights were the busiest the boys had ever known, and there was no time for them to think of their rivalry over the cabin boy's position. Under the guidance of Professor Ploozer, the two young men—along with others studying for the trip to Earth—went from cave to cave, classroom to classroom, test to test, lecture to lecture.

They made field trips to such remote places as the Sea of Serenity and to such busy places as Clavius, the largest crater city in existence. They drew charts, collected rocks, measured radio-activity, and learned the deadly properties of oxygen and the waste caused by water—in preparation for meeting such dangerous elements on Earth.

They even ventured out onto the Moon's surface during the day in an experiment to acquaint the crew with the rays of the sun. Professor Ploozer remarked, with his sly little smile, "'I caught cosmos years ago, and I feel gefine."

To Matt, the most interesting part of the course was spent at the Mooniversity observatory. Studying the heavens, they saw that the sky was a deep black, both night and day. The Sun was a blue-white disk with rosy billows of gas projecting from its edges. Stars were visible in all parts of the sky.

"I caught cosmos years ago and I feel gefine."

Earth appeared as a bluish globe with brilliant white caps at either end. It reflected a good deal of light, but on some occasions it blotted out the sun and became a large black disk with a bright, silvery ring around its rim. To everyone this was a fascinating sight—the big Earth hanging there so close—for it was their target, their destination. They asked Professor Ploozer many questions, which he attempted to answer.

"Sir, why go to the Earth at all if there is no life there?" someone asked.

"That is a good gequestion,"the famous astronomer replied. "Well, there are still things about the place that would be of interest to science. Like a piece from a gejigsaw puzzle. You wouldn't throw it away if you couldn't fit it right away, would you?"

"No," everyone murmured.

"So we study Earth, that peculiar planet, and we come back with gepieces, like a sample of oxygen, which makes you ill if you breathe it but which might be put to some use here. Or like gewater, which we know from observation eats away what it touches, but which might be tamed and made to work for good on the Moon. Another thing, because Earth is bigger, the gepull of gravity is greater; maybe we can learn something about conquering velocipitis by studying that. So we put it all together and maybe we solve the gepuzzle."

"Then why haven't we explored the Earth before this, Professor Ploozer?" Matt asked.

"Ah, my boy, that is what we call the getough one. I will only say that there is a strong anti-Earth group which is against spending money to explore a dead planet. Led by Doctor Robinson K. Russo, they have agreed to this voyage on one condition: that while we are there collecting scientific specimens, we will study ways and means of destroying Earth. Because, as you know, the thing is always in the way, so to speak, and many Moon inhabitants would like to be rid of such an eyesore. Any more questions?"

Matt was congratulating himself on having asked such a fine question when he looked across the classroom and noticed Hector stirring. The

45

big show-off, Matt said to himself. Then Hector's hand shot up. Ploozer pointed to him. "Yes?"

"Say, Prof, what does the *Moon* look like from the *Earth*, hey?"

"Well, um, Hornbloomer"—the professor had trouble with names—"that is something you will find out when you get there. Ho! Ho! And then you can tell me when you come back. Now, everyone, prepare for tomorrow's final examination and the gechoosing of the crew."

As they all filed out of the classroom, Hector whispered into Matt's ear, with that huge super-smile of his, "I'll tell you too, Skinny, when I get back."

"Like fish you will, Fatty," Matt shot back. His ears were burning as he walked away, and he thought he wanted to go on the expedition more than he had ever wanted anything in his whole life.

"If Hector goes," he told himself, "I'll never look at the Earth again!"

IV

Hector Spills the Beans

"How did it go, Matt?" Mr. Looney greeted his son at the cave door as he returned from Copernicus. The boy sat down and told his mother and father everything about the difficult nine days and nights of work.

"Now," he concluded, "I have to sit and wait for them to decide. Gee! If that Hector Hornblower gets it!" He pounded his fist on his knee.

The days seemed endless until one week later the news came. It was good news. The cabin boy on the *Moonbeam II* would be Matthew M. Looney of Crater Plato! Even Matt's mother, who worried, was proud; Matt's father, who preferred the powder works for his son, was pleased; and Matt's sister, who didn't really care, boasted to her friends.

That very night Uncle Lucky came by and spent a long time telling Matt how to prepare for the expedition.

"You won't be able to take much, son. You're not going to the Moonshine Towers for a vacation, you know. Your heavy boots and gloves, and your protective uniform and head-gear, will be provided by the EEF, the Earth Expeditionary Force, which is sponsoring the thing. As you know, we take off Marsday night from the Sea of Crisis. I'll meet you at the Plato Airport, and we'll go on up by molacopter."

By Marsday, after much packing and repacking, Matt seemed to be ready. He had just stuffed a notebook and pencils into the valise—for he planned to keep a log of his journey—and had forced it shut. Now he was giving Maria last-minute instructions about feeding Ronald, the murtle. He felt a lump rise in his throat.

"Good-by, friend," he said to Ronald. He

48

turned to his sister. "Now, don't forget, a spoonful of Cricket Ration in the evening and a saucer of canal juice in the morning."

"I'll try to remember."

"Try to remember!" Matt echoed her words. "You've got to remember!" He scratched Ronald's neck. "You know, I ought to take you with me, and then I wouldn't have to worry about you. After all, I did promise you. That was way back when I didn't think there was a chance I would go to Earth."

"Matt!" his sister cried. "Uncle Lucky said you couldn't take Ronald!"

Matt looked at Maria with his eyes squinting. "Listen. You'd better not say anything."

Just then there was a shout from another part of the cave. "Matthew! Come on! We must leave for the airport."

Matt and Maria stared at each other. Her mouth was open and her eyes were popping. "B-b-but, Matt . . ."

"You just remember to feed him, that's all," Matt growled at her. He swung her around and

49

pushed her out the door ahead of him. He stood alone in the room. He looked sadly at Ronald, picked up his valise, and started out of the room. He paused a moment with his hand on the doorknob.

"Matthew!" the cry was urgent. "We are late!"

"I'm coming! I'm coming!" Matt ran back into his room; he grabbed the little murtle in the palm of his hand and stuck it inside his shirt. Then he ran through the hall to the front door, where his parents were waiting.

A few hours later the boy was looking down on such grand sights as the rugged Caucasian Mountains and the smooth Sea of Serenity while Captain Looney piloted the molacopter toward the distant Sea of Crisis and the main base of the EEF. Matt had almost forgotten about Ronald, who was just a hard little ball next to his master's skin. After they had landed, and the excitement of the flight was over, Matt felt the murtle's tail tickling him, and then he regretted his rash decision to bring the creature along.

He looked sadly at Ronald . . .

A moment later, however, he forgot Ronald again, for there before them was the beautiful spaceship *Moonbeam II.*

"There she is," Captain Looney said with pride. The ship was poised on its launching platform, pointed toward the heavens. In general shape it was circular and fairly flat, with portholes dotting the rim all the way around. Away up high Matt could see the cockpit, a slight projection from the smooth surface of the sleek black ship. At the other end were fins and stabilizing surfaces, and fitting snugly below them were the rocket motors which would send *Moonbeam II* to the Earth and back again.

"I can hardly believe I'm going, Uncle Lucky," Matt said. At that moment he saw a familiar figure walking toward them. It was Professor Ploozer, who would supervise from the control center while the ship was being launched, and who would take charge of the communications between the Moon and the ship during the entire voyage.

While the scientist was still out of hearing,

"There she is," Captain Looney said with pride.

In the control room

Matt's uncle whispered, "By the way, Matt, from now on I'm not your uncle, but your commander. You'll deal with me as Captain Looney, and I'll treat you as a member of the crew."

"Yes, Unc—, I mean, yes, sir."

"Well, gentlemen, gegreetings to EEF headquarters," said the professor. He shook hands with them both and led them to the huge cave where the control center was located.

Matt saw that the place was filled with all kinds of electronic equipment. He was looking it over with great interest when Captain Looney said, "Matt, report to the crew's supply room and pick up your gear. Then proceed to the gangway for inspection."

Captain Looney and Ploozer went away together to check some last-minute details, and a few minutes later Matt found himself standing beneath the spaceship, with his valise in one hand and his helmet, uniform, and other equipment in the other. With him were about twenty other men, who made up the rest of the crew. After a long wait, they saw Captain Looney approaching.

"All right, men, fall in!" ordered the Captain. "Now, you have all been through the dry run so many times that I am sure you know your duties. We take off in a few minutes, so board ship and get to your stations." As the crew filed aboard, Captain Looney turned to Professor Ploozer, who was standing next to him.

"Well, Captain, good luck," said the professor, as they shook hands.

"Thanks, Professor. Keep an eye on us." Looney turned, climbed the ladder, and pulled the hatch closed behind him. He was the last man aboard.

Professor Ploozer walked quickly back to the shelter of the control center, where he seated himself before the huge visual reproduction screen and snapped out, "Start engines!"

A few minutes later, after the countdown, there was a tremendous roar and the *Moonbeam II* —as seen on the screen—was engulfed in dust and smoke. When that had cleared, the ship was gone. Cheers echoed through the control center.

This very scene was also witnessed by anyone on the Moon who could get near a visual reproduction set. The Looneys sat in their living room, watching tensely, and when the cheers rang out, Mrs. Looney wept. Mr. Looney put his arm on her shoulders and comforted her, but she kept on crying.

"Maria," her father said, "why don't you go out and play, dear?"

Because everyone wanted to see the take-off, the VR set was tuned to Channel 14, causing Maria to miss her favorite show, *The Green Cheese Room*. She walked out into the street pouting. There, whom should she run into but Hector Hornblower. Feeling sorry for herself, Maria decided to heckle Hector.

"Matt just went to the Earth. He's the cabin boy, you know."

Hector, in no mood for this, heckled back.

"Say, if my uncle was the pilot and my father's friend was in charge, I bet I'd be cabin boy. I bet—I bet even a *murtle* would be cabin boy."

"Oh, is that so?" Maria stuck her chin out.

"Well, it so happens that Ronald *is*——" She stopped and put her hand to her mouth. Hector's eyes blazed. "Ronald is *what?*"

"Nothing." Maria backed away.

Hector grabbed her tightly. "Did Matt take Ronald with him? Answer me!"

Maria started to cry. "I don't know. He—he promised Ronald, and when I went to feed him, well, he's gone!" She blubbered and ran down the street, exercising the most careful knee action (as she had recently been taught).

Hector stood there for several minutes. The big grin on his face seemed to get bigger. He stared up at the black sky, where he could see the red exhausts of the *Moonbeam II* as the vehicle made its way toward the void. Suddenly he jumped on his micycle and raced home. He threw down the micycle and darted into the cave and into his own room.

"Where in the universe are you running to, son?" his mother asked.

"No place, Mom," he yelled, and slammed the door to his room.

He grabbed pen and paper . . .

There he jerked open the desk drawer and grabbed pen and paper. He printed carefully:

Professor T. P. Ploozer
Earth Expeditionary Force
Sea of Crisis
Dear Professor Ploozer,
  You remember me. I was taking the exams at the Mooniversity. Well, there is something I think you should know about, concerning a fellow on the Earth expedition who is supposed to be cabin boy. His name is Matt Looney and he has a murtle. Now I don't want to start anything, but the murtle is missing and the Looney boy told his sister . . .

Hector wrote for a long time. Finally he signed his name, after finishing the letter. He stamped and addressed the envelope, jumped on his micycle, and sped right to the post office, where he mailed it.

V

Exploring the Earth

*Late Sunday night: I looked back, thought I saw
Crater Plato. Rest of men up forward watching Earth
come closer. Must go now. Time for canal juice on
bridge.*

Matt closed his notebook with a snap and put
it in the drawer beneath the bunk in his small but
tidy cabin. Then he sneaked a look at Ronald,
who was sleeping comfortably hidden under the
pillow. A few minutes later Matt made his way
to the galley, picked up the pitcher of cold canal
juice, and climbed the ladder to the bridge. As he

entered, he heard his uncle speaking to all the officers, who were gathered around him:

"Gentlemen, I have opened our sealed orders, and they direct us to land at the spot known as the South Pole. There, we shall be protected from the rays of the sun, and the temperature is much more bearable than in the hot, unattractive green-and-blue areas of the Earth."

Captain Looney paused, removed his spectacles, and looked up at the group before him. He continued, "Now, men, I believe I have a surprise for you. We are specifically ordered to make a thorough search for any form of life on the planet Earth!"

There was a dramatic silence. All that could be heard was the drone of the rocket engines. Matt felt his heart give a little jump. Finally one of the men addressed the commander.

"Sir, why was this a part of the secret order? I mean, why did they tell us we were just supposed to collect oxygen and water samples and that sort of thing?"

Matt saw his uncle hesitate a moment and then

62

"I have opened our sealed orders . . ."

reply carefully. "Well, I guess I can be frank. I am sure you all know about the Robinson K. Russo Anti-Earth League. This powerful group was able to block the expedition until we agreed that its mission would be to figure out how to move the Earth from its present location, even if it means destroying it.

"As you surely know, this would make further scientific exploration of the planet rather difficult. However, Professor Ploozer and I and other scientists publicly agreed, so that we could get our expedition off the ground. Privately, though, we all feel sure that there is a chance of finding life on Earth, and we want to make that the main purpose of the voyage. If we succeed, we shall have saved Earth and also have delivered a real challenge to the Russo group. I am counting on you all to do your best. That is all."

The men broke up, drinking canal juice as Matt offered it to them, and soon drifted away to their stations, leaving Matt and his uncle alone except for the helmsman and navigator.

"While you're here, Matt, I want to say that I

expect you to take part in the exploration of the Earth. With your curiosity and interest, you ought to be able to make some useful observations for us. Take your notebook with you and keep your eyes open."

"Yes, sir," Matt said.

When his uncle turned away to give full attention to the control panel, Matt gathered together the cups and saucers. As he left the bridge with his tray, he heard a crackling over the inter-spatial network:

"Captain Looney. Space-o-gram from Professor Ploozer. Are you there?"

Matt listened to his uncle acknowledge, but he was soon out of range and heard no more. If he had known the contents of the message, he might not have walked so gaily down the ladder and into the galley. He greeted the cook, Wonder-von Brown, with a big grin.

"Guess what, Mr. Brown, I'm going to help explore the Earth with the others. They really believe there is life there, and we are all to look until we find it."

Wondervon Brown, a big shaggy-haired man wearing a white apron, grunted, then spoke in a foreign accent. "You never find it."

"What do you mean?"

"I tell dem for years dere are people on Earth. Dey don't listen to me. Dey make me cook to shut me up."

"I don't understand, Mr. Brown," Matt said, puzzled.

"Look, my poy," Wondervon Brown waved a soupspoon, "I tell you de people on Earth live up around where it's plue und green. Dey don't live where it's white, where *we* look for dem. But it's okay. You joost go ahead look for dem. I go ahead make moonballs for lunch."

Matt walked away, smiling and shaking his head over Wondervon Brown's ideas. He prepared another canal juice tray, this one for the men in the engine room. He balanced it carefully as he worked his way along the main passageway toward the rear of the ship. By pressing his face against the porthole glass, he could see the Moon in the distance. It had grown smaller, but he

66

"I tell dem for years dere are people on earth.

could still make out landmarks such as the large craters and mountain ranges.

Then Matt turned his attention to Earth and he whistled with surprise. It was enormous. Parts of it were hidden by big puffs of white, and the rest seemed to be many different colors. Matt's excitement grew as he thought of setting foot on the strange planet. He finally tore himself away from the interesting sight and began the descent of the ladder to the engine room.

As he entered, the noise was deafening and there seemed to be steam and smoke everywhere. Men were busy turning valves and reading dials at the main control desk, where he set down the tray.

"Thanks, son!" the chief engineer shouted, as he poured himself a big cup of canal juice. "This is the kind of fuel we really need for a trip to the Earth." He smiled and gulped it down. One by one the other men in the gang came and drank their fill, while Matt looked curiously at the tanks, pipes, wheels, and big engines that sped the *Moonbeam II* through space. He had seen the engine room several times before, but it still fascinated him.

Matt gathered up the things, returned to the galley with his tray, and went off duty.

"Might as well stop and see how Ronald is," he thought to himself, as he worked his way along the passage from the galley. He turned down a small corridor and came to the entrance to his cabin. He opened the door and stopped short. Someone was sitting on his bunk. It was Uncle Lucky! He was not smiling.

"But, Uncle—Captain Looney—sir," stammered Matt. "You're here?"

"Yes, I'm here, Matt," answered his uncle. "But I wish I were not." He held a piece of paper in his hand. "This is a space-o-gram I received, and it says something about a murtle. Shall I read it to you?"

Matt's insides seemed to flip. How did they find out, he asked himself. "No," he replied to Captain Looney. "I know what it probably says." He took Ronald out from under the pillow and

Matt had never felt more miserable in his whole life.

held the animal in the palm of his hand. His uncle just stared at the little creature, not saying anything. "Honest, Uncle Lucky," Matt went on, "I didn't mean anything . . ."

His uncle interrupted him. "I'm sure you think you have a good reason for breaking the rule against bringing pets along, and I don't care to hear about it now. As your uncle, I might be able to forgive you. But as commander, it puts me in a bad spot, having my own nephew disobey orders, showing a lack of discipline for the rest of the crew to see."

Matt had never felt more miserable in his whole life.

"It's little things like this," Looney continued, "that can mean the difference between a career in space and a lifetime in the powder works."

He let this sink in for a moment, and then went on with the lecture. "You have probably learned your lesson, and since only a few of us know about the animal, we'll just keep it to ourselves and concentrate on the more important business of exploring Earth. I expect you to make up for your mistake, Matthew, by doing the best job possible. Let's hope we return to the Moon with something more exciting than a stowaway murtle." He patted Matt's shoulder and went out.

The boy looked at Ronald for a few moments, tucked him away, climbed into his bunk, and tried to go to sleep. He did sleep, because the next thing he knew he was being awakened by the ship's alarm. He jumped out of bed and dressed quickly, knowing that this was the climax of the journey—they would soon reach Earth.

Matt was hurrying out of the room when he thought of Ronald.

"I can't leave him here," he told himself. "If he wakes up, he'll crawl out and someone will surely find him. Well, come on, Mr. Murtle, it's Earth for you too." He stuck the creature into a big side pocket in his spacesuit, fitted his protective helmet on his head, seized his notebook, and reported to the main deck as he heard the loudspeakers blare:

"This is your Captain speaking! We are approaching Earth! Stand by for a landing! Ex-

He stuck the creature into a big side pocket in his space suit . . .

ploration crews report to main deck hatchway!"

There was a slight bump, and *Moonbeam II* was resting on Earth, having delivered the first living persons in the Universe to visit this uninhabited planet. After checking his breathing tanks, which would supply him with vacuum and protect him from the oxygen, Matt climbed down the gangway and put his foot on Earth.

Captain Looney, who had been the first one out, was there directing explorers in various tasks. Speaking through the interhelmetary telephone, he ordered Matt to take Sector B-104 on the chart and to collect samples of the soil that he would find there. Other members of the expedition were moving off in various directions, taking containers, pumps, and other equipment to help them gather what they laughingly called "pieces for Ploozer's gejigsaw gepuzzle."

Actually the men weren't laughing at this moment, for they had to use all their strength to walk and to pull and carry their equipment. Everything, including their feet, seemed about five times as heavy as back home.

74

"There's no danger of velocipitis here," one man grunted to another as he struggled along.

Matt, luckily, didn't have as much to carry as some of the others, but he still found it rough going. It took him an hour to find Sector B-104. Matt kneeled down to inspect the ground. Off to one side of him was a broad expanse of the liquid known as water; on the other side was a high mountain covered with the deposits that made this part of the planet appear white from the Moon. The area where he kneeled seemed to Matt to be a mixture of different unknown minerals.

The boy worked busily for a long time, filling the little tubes with samples and marking them carefully as to location, time, etc. In his notebook he wrote down many comments and descriptions of the things he saw, but he found no evidence that there was anything living in the vicinity. It was after long hours of work that Matt reached to put his pencil away in his pocket. He realized with horror that his pocket was empty.

Ronald was missing!

Frantically Matt searched back and forth, retracing his steps. At last he came upon the place where the murtle must have fallen from his pocket, and from there Matt followed the creature's tracks—the tiny, little footprints straddling the line caused by the dragging tail. The trail seemed to go on and on, closer and closer to the water. Finally it stopped completely, as though some mysterious hand had simply lifted the animal into the atmosphere. A few feet away was the edge of the water, but the tracks stopped abruptly short of it.

Ronald the murtle had disappeared.

As Matt stood there, wondering what to do, he heard himself being called over the interhelmetary phone: "Cadet Looney, return to the *Moonbeam* at once!"

"Oh, poor Ronald," the boy muttered to himself as he pushed his way back to the landing area. "He's probably dead by now, breathing all that oxygen." His eyes itched as he cried the way they do on the Moon—without tears.

VI

A Crash Landing on the Moon

Approaching the *Moonbeam*, Matt saw Captain Looney waiting for him.

"Matt," he said, "I called you back because I wanted your report on what you've found. I hope it's favorable."

"Briefly, sir, no. I collected most of my samples, but I found no evidence of any living things of any kind."

Captain Looney looked away with a pained expression on his face. "It looks as though our trip has been a failure, then, son. All the teams have brought back the same report. Well, let's

77

hope we get an A for effort, anyway." He looked at his watch. "We have a few hours before take-off. Guess I'll take a nap."

"Sir." Matt spoke up as his uncle started away. "May I have permission to do a little more exploring? There are a few loose ends I'd like to clear up."

"Of course, Matt, go right ahead."

Elated, Matt plodded back to the spot where he had lost Ronald. "I guess it wasn't a fib," he thought, "to call Ronald 'a few loose ends.'"

One hour later he was standing at the place where Ronald's tracks stopped abruptly. Then Matt noticed another strange thing: the water's edge, which had been several feet from the murtle tracks when he last saw them, was now lapping the spot where the tracks ended. Puzzled, Matt stood there. Then he observed a slight movement in the water. A shiny black object slowly emerged, shedding drops of water off its back. It moved slowly onto dry land, leaving a trail of little pawprints and tailmarks. It was the murtle.

"Ronald!" the boy cried, bending to pick him up. "Are you all right? Let me look at you!" Ronald seemed in the best of health and, in fact, cleaner than he had ever been.

"That's funny," Matt thought. "If the oxygen didn't hurt him, the water should have finished him off." As he tucked the pet back into his spacesuit pocket, Matt tried to figure out how the murtle could have survived. He decided to make a record of everything. He took out his notebook, sat down, and began to write:

> Strange happenings on Earth. How Ronald the murtle breathed oxygen and went into the water but lived. I first noticed the murtle tracks after I had been studying Sector B-104 . . .

For quite some time Matt wrote, drew maps and sketches, and checked the conclusions he came to. As he finished, he heard himself paged: "Cadet Looney, return to *Moonbeam*. We take off in one hour."

Matt packed up all his things, made sure he had Ronald in his pocket, and went back to the spaceship. Soon he was in his cabin removing his exploration equipment and hiding Ronald beneath the pillow again. He lay down on his bunk hoping Captain Looney would forget about the tiny stowaway by the time they reached home.

"I wonder if I should tell Uncle Lucky about Ronald coming out of the water?" Matt asked himself. "Maybe I'd better not bring it up at all."

The next few days were so busy for the cabin boy that he had little time to see his uncle or even to feed the murtle regularly. On the last night of the return trip he wished he had been more watchful.

Matt was in his bunk when the smooth flight of the *Moonbeam II* was broken by a violent jerk. The spaceship seemed to twist around in all directions, tossing Matt out of his bunk and sending the loose objects in the cabin flying against the walls and ceiling. The frightened boy knew what had happened: they had lost their gravity!

"Emergency stations!" cried the loudspeakers. Matt quickly dressed and rushed to his station on the bridge. He had to pull himself along by grasping the handrails and going hand over hand. He

He had to pull himself along by grasping the handrails . . .

passed men who were going in the opposite direction, and they had to sort of climb over each other. All the time the ship was out of control, spinning and twisting. Matt's feet kept slipping this way and that, and it was only after the greatest effort that he reached his place.

There he saw that the helmsman and navigator had made themselves fast to their seats and were struggling without success to bring the ship under some control. Captain Looney and the other officers were holding on to railings with one hand, while their bodies seemed to flop around in all directions.

"Matt!" gasped his uncle. "See if you can get down to the Artificial Gravity Locker, where the repair crews are, and have them give you an estimate of how long it will be before they fix this trouble."

Matt, being the smallest man in the crew, could move more easily than the others. He pulled his way down two decks below, where he saw a gang of men trying to hold themselves close enough to the Artificial Gravity Machine to work on it. He spoke to the chief repairman.

"When will you have her fixed? Captain wants to know."

"Can't tell, son. Something's gotten into the fuse box, and we can't even find it yet. Tell him we're doing our best."

Matt forced his way back to the bridge with this message. He found that the other officers had strapped themselves down. But the real danger had only begun, as Matt realized when he heard the commander speak.

"We can't land in this condition, men. How are we fixed for fuel, Mr. Bones?" he asked the first mate.

"We can make one pass but that's all, sir."

"Well, make it, then. We're due to land in a few minutes; but if we go in like this, we'll wreck the ship and ourselves too."

Matt and the others on the bridge rattled and shook along with the *Moonbeam II* while they circled the Moon. The time seemed endless as

83

they waited to hear from the repairmen at the Artificial Gravity Locker. But only too soon they had completed the pass and were approaching the landing platform at the Sea of Crisis again!

Mr. Bones looked at Captain Looney. "The tanks are empty, sir."

Captain Looney looked grim. Then he turned and gave the order: "Take her in! Mr. Bones, alert the crew to prepare for a crash landing."

No sooner had he spoken these words than there was a cheer from afar. At the same time the men on the bridge heard a familiar whine as the wheels of the Artificial Gravity Machine started up again. In seconds, they found their feet planted firmly on the deck, with nothing more than a headache to remind them of what they had been through.

Captain Looney, Matt, and everyone else sighed in relief, smiling broadly at their narrow escape. Their grins disappeared almost immediately, though, when the rocket engines sputtered and stopped. Captain Looney grabbed the wheel from the helmsman.

Captain Looney grabbed the wheel from the helmsman.

"Here, I'll take over! Men, we're going to glide her in! There's just enough momentum! Hold on!"

The experienced pilot expertly moved the wheel this way and that, adjusting the fins and stabilizers with the foot controls. The great ship was completely silent, and it gave Matt an eerie sensation to see the surface of the Moon come closer. Finally there was a gentle bump and a slight scraping noise. All was still for a minute. Then the crew broke out in cheers.

Mr. Bones turned to Matt. "You have just seen why they call him the greatest spaceman in the Universe, son."

Matt stood there proudly, watching the officers clap his uncle on the back and shake his hand. They were interrupted when two men came onto the bridge and asked to speak to the Captain. Matt saw that one was the chief repairman he had seen at the Artificial Gravity Locker.

"Sir," he said to Captain Looney, "we found out what was wrong with the Artificial Gravity Machine."

86

"We found out what was wrong with the
Artificial Gravity machine."

"Oh, really? What was it?"

"You're not going to believe it, sir."

"Oh, go ahead, man. What's the story?" Captain Looney asked impatiently.

"Well, sir, there was a murtle in the fuse box." He held out his hand and there was Ronald, with his feet and head retracted and only his little tail hanging out, wagging slightly.

Matt couldn't believe his ears. Then he remembered that, in the excitement of the last few nights and days, he had forgotten all about Ronald, and the animal must have slipped away from his hiding place. The other men, shocked, stared at Ronald, knowing that the tiny thing had almost wrecked their spaceship and killed them all.

The next to speak was Captain Looney, who said slowly to his nephew, "Matthew, go to your quarters and remain there until I come to release you. That will be after the crew members have made things shipshape and have debarked. Now, beat it! And take your murtle with you!" He was really angry.

88

Much later Matt sat on his bunk, looking out the porthole at the crowds that had gathered to greet the *Moonbeam*. The crew came down the gangway and were engulfed in the cheering mobs. As he watched them, the door of his cabin opened and his uncle came in and sat down on the bunk.

"I don't know what to say, Matthew. The expedition failed to find life on Earth, and I am sure that my enemies at the Space Academy will be after my head for that. And when they find out that the ship was almost wrecked because my nephew brought along his pet animal, well, there'll never be another expedition to *anyplace*. If there is, I won't be on it." He paused and rubbed his forehead with his fingers.

"Uncle Lucky," Matt said quietly, "all I can do is say I am sorry. I guess I'll never get a chance to be a scientist. But, could I ask you something?"

"Yes, I suppose so," his uncle sighed.

Matt got out his notebook and opened it to the pages where he had described Ronald's adventures on Earth. He showed his uncle the drawings and read to him the notes he had made.

As he went on, Captain Looney showed some interest. Then Matt asked him, "How come the murtle wasn't killed by the oxygen and the water? Do you think maybe there are murtles living on the Earth, or something?"

Captain Looney scratched his head. "I just don't know, son. I'd sure like to have Robinson K. Russo try to answer these questions. The only trouble is, I've already sent my report to the Earth Expeditionary Force. I said we found no evidence on Earth that should arouse our interest at all. The news is all over Moon by now. I really don't see how we can bring up this new material, as small as it is, and expect anyone to notice. Besides, coming from the cabin boy who —well, who caused us so much trouble—it doesn't seem to stand a chance. And there's probably some simple explanation, anyway."

Matt hung his head in despair. His uncle said kindly, "Well, come on, son. We might as well face the crowds of ordinary people out there. They are always glad to see us, even if the big shots aren't."

VII

Trouble Ahead

Every time Captain Lockhard Looney ever returned from one of his dramatic journeys to outer space, he was greeted with the wildest sort of welcome. Apparently this latest venture of his would be no different, for the great pilot-scientist was without doubt the most popular hero of modern times.

Coming down the gangplank at the Sea of Crisis base, Captain Looney and Matt were surrounded by a mob of people, mostly men with microphones, cameras, and other reportorial equipment. They were shouting and shoving and demanding answers to their questions.

"Hey, Captain, is it true you didn't find anything on Earth?"

"Fellows, move over here so we can take your picture, will ya?"

"What's this story about someone smuggling a live animal on board?"

"What kind of a landing was that, Captain?"

The confusion was so great that Matt couldn't make head or tail of it. He moved on toward the control center cave and the crew lockers, where he would leave his special supplies and prepare to return home. Ronald was safely put away inside the valise.

It was then that Matt saw the picket line. A row of policemen was on hand to maintain order, to hold back the crowds of shouting, surging people who carried signs on which were written such messages as: *Captain Loonacy Misses Again* and *Let Ploozer Have Earth—We'll Take Moon.*

The boy pushed his way through the mob and into the control room. There he found Professor

Men with microphones, cameras, and other reportorial equipment

Ploozer sitting sadly on a calculating machine.

"What's the matter, Professor?"

The old man slapped his bald head with his hand. "Oh, my boy, if you only knew! Well, the expedition is a gefailure, that's what's the matter. Came back empty-gehanded, that's what. Oh, Captain Looney will be all right. He'll go on visual reproduction and be interviewed. He's a big hero. But me—the Mooniversity wants to know why I sent the party to Earth if there is nothing there. It cost plenty of mooney, I can tell you."

He slapped his head some more and suddenly burst out, "And you didn't help any, boy, taking that gemurtle with you! Oh, oh . . ." He shuffled out of the room, groaning.

Matt packed his things and waited in the locker room for his uncle to come along. When the Captain did come in, he was smiling.

"My, that was a grand welcome, wasn't it, son? All those reporters. Just like old times."

"But, Uncle Lucky, did you see the picket line?"

94

"Yes," the officer looked up from unlacing his boots, "but that's nothing. There are always some soreheads around, screaming about taxes or something. Listen, Matt," he waved a boot at his nephew, "if you're always thinking about saving mooney, you're never going to get anything done on this Moon. You've got to think big!" He finished changing his clothes, and soon he was standing in the full-dress uniform of the Space Navy, with all his medals and awards stretched across his chest.

"All right, let's go! Wait till you see the welcome they give us back at good old Crater Plato!"

A few hours later, with Captain Looney at the controls, the molacopter hovered over the Plato Airport. A huge crowd was gathered below.

"Look at 'em!" the happy officer cried. "They won't give us room to land! There, the crater cops have pushed 'em aside. All right, here we come!" He stuck his head outside and smiled.

The 'copter dropped down to the ground and was immediately swept up in the tide of humanity. The cheers and shouts were deafening. With

The Sky Medal with Lava Cluster

great difficulty the cops found room for the two passengers to make their way to the airport cave, where more photographers and reporters and crater officials awaited them.

The mayor of Crater Plato stepped forward. "Captain Lockhard Looney, I hereby decorate you with the Order of the Distinguished Space-man, First Class." He pinned something on the officer's blouse, not blinking an eye when he noticed that Captain Looney already had an ODS, First Class, which he had won when he circled the Sun four years earlier.

The mayor then turned to Matt. "And for another of our local heroes, Matthew Looney, I award you the Sky Medal, with Lava Cluster, for your feat." He attached a shiny object to the boy's shirt. "And now for the triumphal march!"

The next thing the bewildered and excited boy knew, he was seated between the mayor and his uncle in the back seat of the official car. They were moving slowly down Canal Street in the midst of a shower of powder falling from the roofs and windows of the buildings on both sides.

This was the traditional powder parade welcome for homecoming heroes, an event Matt had never witnessed—except on the VR screen. And here he was, a part of it. It was almost more than he could stand!

It was a tired and happy boy who stepped out of the powder-covered vehicle in front of his home cave in Plato. Captain Looney, grinning happily, got out with him, and they both thanked the crater officials who had given them the fine welcome. As the car drove away, Matt and his uncle walked toward the front door, wondering where the Looney family could be.

"Why aren't they here to meet us?" Matt asked.

"I don't know, son; maybe they are still watching us on the VR set."

"How can they watch us there—when we're right here?"

They both laughed. Just then the front door opened and Mrs. Looney stood there, staring at them with a frightened look on her face.

"Well, Diana, I told you I'd bring him back," Uncle Lucky said.

"Did you see the parade, Mother?"

With that the woman turned and ran into the cave, covering her face with her hands. Matt and his uncle followed, puzzled by her actions. Entering the living room, they saw Matt's father in conversation with two men in uniform. Matt saw that the uniforms were similar to Captain Looney's, but with different markings. They were obviously officers of high rank, because the Captain jumped to attention when he saw them.

"At ease, Looney," one of the officers ordered. "Now that your public is finished with you, we have a little matter to discuss. Reports have come in to Space Navy High Command that the discipline on your recent trip was lax, and below the standards required on official flights. This unfortunate business of the murtle is a good example. I understand this is the boy here, and that he is related to you, too." He pointed to Matt.

The other officer spoke up. "Space Navy Headquarters have started an investigation to find out what's behind all this, and why this wasteful voyage was made to the useless planet Earth. It is my duty, then, to inform you that a Court of Inquiry will meet tomorrow night at SNHQ. You, Captain Lockhard Looney, will be there prepared to tell your side of the story."

Captain Looney made no reply except to say, "Yes, sir."

The first officer spoke again. "Furthermore, since the key issue in the inquiry is the matter of the murtle running loose on board the *Moonbeam II*——"

Matt jumped up. "He wasn't running loose! He was ——"

"Silence!" the officer barked out. Then he continued, "—the murtle running loose on board the *Moonbeam II* and damaging the spaceship, and endangering the crew, therefore the boy Matthew Looney and his animal known as Ronald the murtle are hereby ordered to attend the hearing, with whatever evidence is necessary."

The men marched out, leaving all the Looneys sitting there gloomily. Finally Uncle Lucky shook his fist at the closed door and cried, "Those

"A Court of Inquiry will meet tomorrow night . . ."

bums!" Then he fell back into his chair and sat silently with his chin in his hands. Mrs. Looney wept softly.

After a long time Matt saw his uncle pull himself up in his chair and turn his head toward him. "Say, Matt," he said slowly, "what was that you were telling me on the spaceship about the murtle on Earth?"

"Well, Uncle Lucky, it was just about how Ronald went into the water and came out again. It's all in my notebook."

"Why didn't you show me the notebook?"

"Gee, I did, Uncle Lucky. You were right there in my cabin——"

"Oh, yes, I seem to recall something like that. I guess I wasn't too sharp right then, after that landing. Well, you know, I've been thinking. If the murtle wasn't killed by oxygen and water, maybe there are some living beings that *can* survive under such conditions. Hmm."

"Yes, that's what I was telling you!" Matt burst out.

102

"Oh, were you? And you say it's all in that notebook? Well, supposing we fire a few of those questions at *them*, instead of having them fire questions at us? What do you say, boy? Are you willing to make a fight of it?"

"Oh, yes, sir!" Matt cried eagerly.

His uncle jumped up out of his chair so suddenly that velocipitis sent him up to the ceiling, where he gave his head a crack.

"Ouch!" he said, rubbing the spot. He pushed on the ceiling and forced his way down to the floor again. He started for the door. "We'll lick this thing, Matt, don't you worry. You be there at the hearing. Bring Ronald, and don't forget your notebook. 'By, everyone." He walked out.

Alone with his parents for the first time since his return, Matt didn't know what to say. At last his mother smiled and came over and kissed him.

"We're glad to see you back, Matt, no matter what's happened."

"Yes, son," his father said. "You were foolish to take the animal with you, but you've certainly learned your lesson now, and I'm not going to make it any worse for you. I want you to know I'm on your side in this battle."

He stopped and looked at Mrs. Looney. "I'm afraid, though, this means the end for poor Lucky. The jealous admirals at headquarters have been after his skin for years."

Matt went to his room, where he pulled the murtle from the valise and placed him in his cage. "Well, Ronald, a lot has happened since I took you out of this room. And I guess it isn't all over yet."

Ronald looked at Matt and wagged his tail, which is a murtle's way of saying he is hungry.

VIII

The Trial

"Will Hector Hornblower please take the witness stand!"

Matt, sitting in the first row of the courtroom, twisted around to see Hector's head bobbing up and down as he came along the aisle. He appeared in the front of the room and took his seat in the witness chair, facing the spectators. Beside him was the bench where sat the three admirals who were running the investigation.

The trial had been going on all night, and many witnesses had come forth to show that the *Moonbeam II* had cost a lot of mooney, that the trip to Earth had been a complete waste of time, and that no evidence of life at all had been discovered. There had also been testimony that Captain Looney had failed to enforce discipline. Seated next to him, Matt could see a slight smile on his uncle's face. "Got the notebook, boy?" he whispered in Matt's ear. Matt patted the book. "It's all right here," he whispered back.

"Now, Hector," the Chief Investigator was saying, "don't be nervous. We are just trying to to find out a few facts. Now, did you write this letter to Professor T. P. Ploozer?"

"Yes, sir." Hector's voice was barely audible.

"Will you tell the Court, in your own words, how it happened."

"Well, I saw Maria and she——"

"Who is Maria, young man?" the voice of the First Admiral boomed out.

"Why, that's Matt's sister. He owns the murtle."

"All right. Proceed."

"So Maria told me he promised him he'd take him to Earth——"

"Now Hector," the Chief Investigator was saying,
"don't be nervous."

"Who promised whom?" the voice boomed out again.

"Matt promised Ronald."

"And who is Ronald?!" the voice was loud enough to hear across the whole universe.

"He's the murtle." Hector then explained how he had happened to write to Professor Ploozer. When he finished, the Chief Investigator faced the bench.

"Your Honors, I wish to enter this letter as Exhibit A." The admirals nodded their heads all together. The Chief Investigator faced the courtroom again and shouted, "Call Matthew Looney to the stand!"

Matt was startled to hear his name called so suddenly. His knees were shaking as he perched on the edge of the witness chair. His uncle winked at him, which cheered him up a bit. The Chief Investigator walked over to a long table that stretched out in the space before the judges' bench. On it he placed the Hornblower letter, Exhibit A, and he picked up an object familiar to Matt. It was Ronald's cage, with Ronald in it,

It was Ronald's cage with Ronald in it . . .

all huddled up inside of his shell with his tail sticking out.

The Investigator held the cage up high for all to see. "Can you identify this?" he asked Matt.

"Yes, sir," the boy replied. "That's Ronald the murtle."

"And this is your pet," the Chief Investigator thrust his face up close to Matt's, "which you carried aboard the spaceship in disobedience of your orders—adding to the confusion of the so-called expedition and almost killing everyone on board?"

"Yes," Matt barely murmured.

On one side of the room there was a lot of noise as the representatives of the press, radio, and visual reproduction agencies took note that here was the murtle that had been to the Earth. It would make a good human-interest story.

"Your Honors," the Chief Investigator announced, "I would like to enter this animal and its cage as Exhibit B." The admirals nodded their heads, and the cage was placed back on the long table.

As Matt went back to his seat, he could see that Ronald was still hidden inside his protective shell. He gave a low, quiet whistle—which was his secret call for Ronald—and he saw the murtle's tail move slightly. He was alive, but hungry.

"Call Robinson K. Russo to the witness stand!" The cry went up just as Matt sat down. He whispered to his father, who was seated by his side, "Why don't they let Uncle Lucky talk?"

His father whispered back. "Because he's too popular. Once he got on the stand, he'd have the audience cheering and he'd tear the trial to pieces."

On the witness stand now was the man Matt had heard so much about but whom he had never seen. Doctor Russo was a small person with a great, big head. He was said to be the only man who could frown all the time and never have it hurt him. On the other hand, they said, if he smiled—*that* caused him pain. This was unusual on the Moon.

"Now, Doctor Russo, you are one of the Moon's foremost experts on outer space, am I right?" the Investigator queried.

Doctor Russo looked proudly around the courtroom, with a big frown on his face.

"I am." The scientist looked proudly around the courtroom, with a big frown on his face.

"Then please tell the Court what you know about the Earth Expeditionary Force and its trip to the dead planet."

"Gladly. In the first place, our Anti-Earth League has in its files all the information anyone would ever want concerning the Earth. Therefore, the only reason we consented to this expedition was that we were led to believe they would find out an easy way to get rid of the nuisance planet. Now it turns out that Captain Looney and the others—under secret orders—spent their precious time there searching for something that does not exist: life on the Earth!"

"Isn't it true, then," the Investigator asked, "that Looney, Ploozer, and gang falsified the facts of the expedition so they could raise mooney to make the trip? And isn't it true that the mooney was wasted because the voyage was a complete failure, mainly due to the lies and bad leadership? Answer yes or no, please."

Before Robinson K. Russo could say anything,

Captain Looney shouted, "I object! How can he answer yes or no to such a question?" The audience cheered and clapped.

"Order in the Court!" boomed the First Admiral, hammering his gavel on the bench. "Captain Looney, be seated! If there is any more disturbance, I shall clear the room of spectators!"

Matt's throat hurt more than he had ever known it to; he was so angry that—before he could stop himself—he stood up and cried, "Sir! I would like to ask Doctor Russo some questions which might clear things up."

The First Admiral's gavel thumped so hard it shook the courtroom. "I have already ruled," he shouted, "that we will have no interruptions and disturbance from people in the room! Let the witness answer the question."

But at that moment the Chief Investigator rushed forward to the bench and engaged the three admirals in a private conference. The four heads huddled together as they conversed in low tones, arguing intensely about something.

Finally they broke off, and the First Admiral

faced the courtroom again. He seemed pleased with himself as he announced, "The Chief Investigator, in an attempt to get at all the facts, has agreed that it might be helpful if some of the witnesses were permitted to ask some questions." He nodded at the Investigator, who stood there smirking. Obviously he had something up his sleeve.

"Your Honors," said the Chief Investigator, "if the cabin boy thinks he can help, let him try." He sat down smugly. Everyone in the courtroom turned their eyes upon Matthew Looney. Doctor Russo allowed himself a quick smile of contempt.

Matt suddenly felt very small and helpless. But his uncle gripped his arm and said, in a low voice, "Go to it, Matt. They're hoping you'll make us all look like fools and spoil our case. Take the notebook and make Robinson K. Russo tell us the answers to those questions. Then we'll see who the fools are."

The boy's knees shook as he approached the front of the room. He opened the book, and all

115

his notes and charts seemed to swim before his eyes. But, miraculously, the pages cleared and a surge of confidence went through him. He faced the witness.

"Doctor," he asked, "does anyone believe there is life on Earth?"

"Not now," the scientist answered.

"Is that because of the deadly oxygen that covers the surface?"

"Yes. And the expedition searched the land area, finding nothing. It was surrounded by water, which causes disintegration, so no living thing could exist there, either."

"Doctor Russo, does a murtle breathe?"

"Certainly, my boy," the man answered.

"Doctor, my murtle was lost for several hours on the Earth, and he was breathing. He wore no protective helmet. He is still alive and healthy. How come?"

"Why, —er, I don't know," the surprised answer came. The admirals looked up, startled. The press table suddenly stopped its activity, and the spectators were quiet, waiting tensely to see what happened next.

Matt looked at his notebook. "Isn't it possible that oxygen is safe to breathe? Do you know of anyone who died from it?"

"Yes—I mean, no. I mean, I don't know."

Matt went on. He showed the scientist his notebook. "Here is a drawing of the murtle tracks on Earth. You see they stop suddenly. Here they start again, where the murtle came *out* of the water. I saw the murtle come out. Why didn't the water kill him?"

"I don't know! He should be dead!" the poor man cried.

There was some confusion at the press table. Three reporters had hurried out of the courtroom. The spectators were on the edge of their seats. Captain Looney and Matt's father were spellbound.

"Another thing," Matt said, showing Doctor Russo his notebook. "I want you to look at my sketches. Here"—he pointed—"is where the murtle tracks stop short, at the place where the creature went into the water. But here"—he pointed again—"a few feet away, is the water's edge as I found it a couple of hours after Ronald had disappeared."

"Yes, son, what is your question?"

"Doesn't that prove that the water moved in the meantime?"

"I have never heard of water moving," the man mumbled, shifting uncomfortably in his chair.

"Well, look here, at this other drawing of the same scene," Matt continued. "This is the way it was some time later when I went back to search for Ronald again. The water's edge was back to where it was when the murtle entered it." Matt held the notebook under Doctor Russo's nose.

"Are you sure?" the scientist asked weakly.

"Of course I'm sure," the boy replied, "because I was there. I made this map when the murtle came out of the water. In other words, in about five or six hours the water's edge moved several

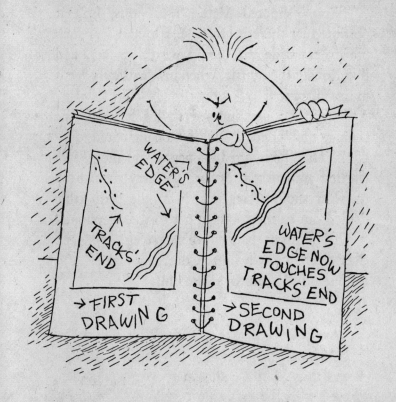

"Doesn't that prove that the water moved in the meantime?"

feet away from this spot and then back to it again!"

"Incredible!" cried the witness.

"Now," shouted Matt, "I ask this! Isn't it possible that there is life on Earth, and that such life exists inside that liquid we call water, and that Ronald the murtle, when lost, naturally went in that direction?"

Captain Looney jumped to his feet, hit the ceiling, and cried, "Oh, if Ronald could only talk!" Then he hugged his nephew as the people cheered and rushed forward to carry them both on their shoulders. The men at the press table dashed out of the room to get to the telephones.

The admirals banged their gavels over and over again, announcing, "Court adjourned!" But no one heard them over the din.

IX

Everyone Gets Promoted

"BOY TOSSES TOUGH QUESTIONS AT SCIENTIST," said the headline of one newspaper.

"MAY BE LIFE ON EARTH AFTER ALL," screamed another. There was a photograph, on the front page, of Matt and Uncle Lucky being carried by the crowds. Underneath, the caption read, "Lucky Looney rides again . . ."

In the Looney cave there was jubilation. Mrs. Looney baked a big cake, and all the Looneys—including Lockhard Looney, the pilot-scientist and hero—sat down and had a party.

121

Monroe Looney said to his son, "Matt, I am really proud of you."

"We all are," added Uncle Lucky. Everyone was smiling almost enough to burst. And sitting in the middle of the table in his cage was Ronald the murtle. His head and paws were all the way out of his shell, showing how happy he was.

Mr. Looney looked at the creature. "Exhibit B, indeed! You showed 'em, Ronald. You know what, Lockhard? The Cricket Ration Company wants to use Ronald's picture on the label of every can. How about that?"

Captain Looney grinned. "Well," he said, looking at his watch, "I must be off to see my superiors."

After Captain Looney had said his farewells and left the cave, Matt stood up. "Well, I must be going too."

"Where to, Matt?" his mother asked, raising her eyebrows.

"No place. G'by." He wandered slowly enough out of the cave; but after he had gotten to the street, he headed quickly in one direction, as though he knew exactly where he was going.

As he went along, he was muttering to himself. "I'm going to give that Hornblower kid the biggest punch in the nose he ever saw! There's his cave now, the big so-and-so."

At that moment the door of the Hornblower cave opened and someone came out and hurried down the street toward Matt. In the dim earthshine Matt could not see who it was, but then he recognized Hector!

"Now I've got you, you big tattletale, bully, and show-off!" he shouted at Hector, and he lunged at him so fast that he knocked the larger boy to the ground. He began to pummel him in the ribs unmercifully.

"Stop, Matt! Ow! Don't! That's enough!" Hector whimpered. Finally Matt had to quit to get his breath back.

"Oh-h-h," groaned Hector. "You really hurt me. I—I was just—coming over to your place. My father gave me a licking and made me promise to apologize." Both boys stood up, Hector holding his ribs and Matt clenching his fists. "No, don't sock me any more, please."

"All right, where's the apology?"

"I didn't mean to do it, Matt. I was mad because you won the trip to Earth. Besides, you were wrong to take the murtle—no, don't punch me again—you were right—it's okay—I'm sorry!"

"Forget it, Hector." Matt dropped his fists and put out a hand. Hector shook it.

"Say, thanks a lot, Matt." Hector grinned at him ."You know, I still can't understand that business about the liquid moving away and then coming back, a few hours later. Do you suppose it just keeps doing it all the time?"

Matt's eyes widened. "That's what I was thinking. You remember when we were at the observatory with Professor Ploozer, when we were taking that course at the Mooniversity?"

Hector nodded.

"And we looked through the telescope at Earth a few times, and each time it seemed that all the blue liquid had changed position?"

"I didn't mean to do it, Matt."

Hector nodded again. "It changes position about every six hours, then," he said.

"Right. So there is life on Earth, after all, and it exists inside the water. How else can you explain the constant movement of the Earth's water, back and forth, day in and day out, month in and month out?"

"The people inside it are moving it, for some reason. Say, Matt, could I come over and see Ronald? Also, I'm supposed to apologize to your folks too."

"Sure, come on." The two walked back toward the Looney home together.

As Matt entered the living room, his mother spoke to him, "Where did you go?"

"Out."

"What did you do?"

"Nothing."

"Well, Matt, while you were gone your Uncle Lucky telephoned. He is bringing over some men who want to talk to you. I don't know what it's all about." Just then Mrs. Looney saw the second figure sneaking in the door. "Well, Hector Hornblower!" she cried. "To think you'd have the NERVE to show your face in THIS cave, after what YOU'VE done!"

"It's all right, Mom," Matt soothed her. "He's here to say he's sorry."

Whereupon Hector made his apologies to Mr. and Mrs. Looney, who quickly forgave him and asked him to have a piece of cake. He sat there munching it and watching Ronald finish up his Cricket Ration. The doorbell rang.

"That must be Uncle Lucky with his friends," said Mr. Looney, getting up and opening the door.

Sure enough, in walked the smiling spaceman, followed by two others in uniform.

"Well, if it isn't the great Captain Looney," said his brother jokingly.

"What do you mean 'Captain'?" he replied, pointing to a shoulder. Everyone rushed forward. There was pinned the insignia of a rear admiral.

"Rear Admiral Looney! Congratulations!" cried his brother.

127

Rear Admiral Looney!

Then, it was time to take note of the two other men who had entered the room. Believe it or not, they were the same two officers who had met Lucky Looney and Matthew on their return from the powder parade. The same two who had notified them of the investigation. For some reason, Matt saw, they were both standing stiffly at attention.

When his uncle barked "At ease, men!" at the two admirals, Matt looked at their uniforms and saw that they were not admirals any more. They were captains.

"Thank you, sir," one of the officers said. "We are here to extend the official apologies of Space Navy Headquarters to Cadet Matthew M. Looney for subjecting him to the recent investigation. We are also here to report that SNHQ has taken over the Earth Expeditionary Force and is making preparations for sending a second party to Earth. This will mainly be for determining the answers to the questions raised by Cadet Looney, regarding life on Earth."

"It is our honor," added the second officer, "to

request that Cadet Looney join the crew of Earth Expedition No. 2 as co-pilot to his uncle, Rear Admiral Looney. If Cadet Looney accepts, he will be promoted to rank of Spaceman, First Class."

"Not if school's on, he can't go on any trips to Earth," Mrs. Looney announced firmly.

"The expedition will be sent during school recess, Mrs. Looney," the officer told her, with a funny look on his face.

"Oh, boy," Matt shouted. "Know what that means? Another trip on the *Moonbeam!* Sure I'll go."

The first officer smiled. "That's fine, son. One slight correction, though. The Navy is building a new and better spaceship to replace the *Moonbeam II.* It's to be called the *Ploozer.*"

Hector had been silent all this time, and Matt had forgotten about him, until he happened to glance his way and saw the boy looking rather sad.

"Just a minute," Matt said. "I'd like to make

130

a request—I'd like to be able to name the cabin boy on the *Ploozer*. May I?" He looked at his uncle.

"Certainly. Who?"

"He's right here. Nəme's Hector Hornblower." He pulled Hector out into the middle of the room. Hector's huge grin was huger than anyone had ever seen it.

"Why not?" asked Rear Admiral Looney. "After all, he's been through the tough Mooniversity training course. I'm sure he'll make a darned good cabin boy."

"Well, isn't that nice of you, sonny," Mrs. Looney said. "Now let's all sit down and finish the cake."

"Yes, and don't forget to take Ronald with you on the next trip so he can show you where to start exploring," little Maria piped up.

Mr. Looney looked at his daughter. "Honey, come over here," he said thoughtfully. "You're not interested in that space stuff, are you? Here, sit on my lap while I tell you about the powder factory. If you're a good girl, maybe some night soon I'll take you over to the Mount Pico Powder Works and show you how much fun you can have there."

Matt and his Uncle Lucky glanced at each other, smiling, but they couldn't say anything because their mouths were full of delicious cake.